Beast Quest®

Lypida The Shadow Fiend

BY ADAM BLADE

ORCHARD

THE NORTHERN MOUNTAINS
THE CENTRAL PLAINS
THE FOREST OF FEAR
GRASSY PLAINS
WESTERN OCEAN
THE CITY OF SNAKES
THE WINDING
SPINDREL
THE RUBY DESERT

WELCOME TO

Collect the special coins in this book.
You will earn one gold coin for
every chapter you read.

Once you have finished all the chapters,
find out what to do with your gold coins at
the back of the book.

With special thanks to Conrad Mason

For Lily Cassap

www.beastquest.co.uk

ORCHARD BOOKS

First published in Great Britain in 2018 by The Watts Publishing Group

1 3 5 7 9 10 8 6 4 2

A CIP catalogue record for this book is available from the British Library.

ISBN 978 1 40834 333 3

Printed in Great Britain

The paper and board used in this book are made from wood from responsible sources

Orchard Books
An imprint of Hachette Children's Group
Part of The Watts Publishing Group Limited
Carmelite House, 50 Victoria Embankment, London EC4Y 0DZ

An Hachette UK Company
www.hachette.co.uk
www.hachettechildrens.co.uk

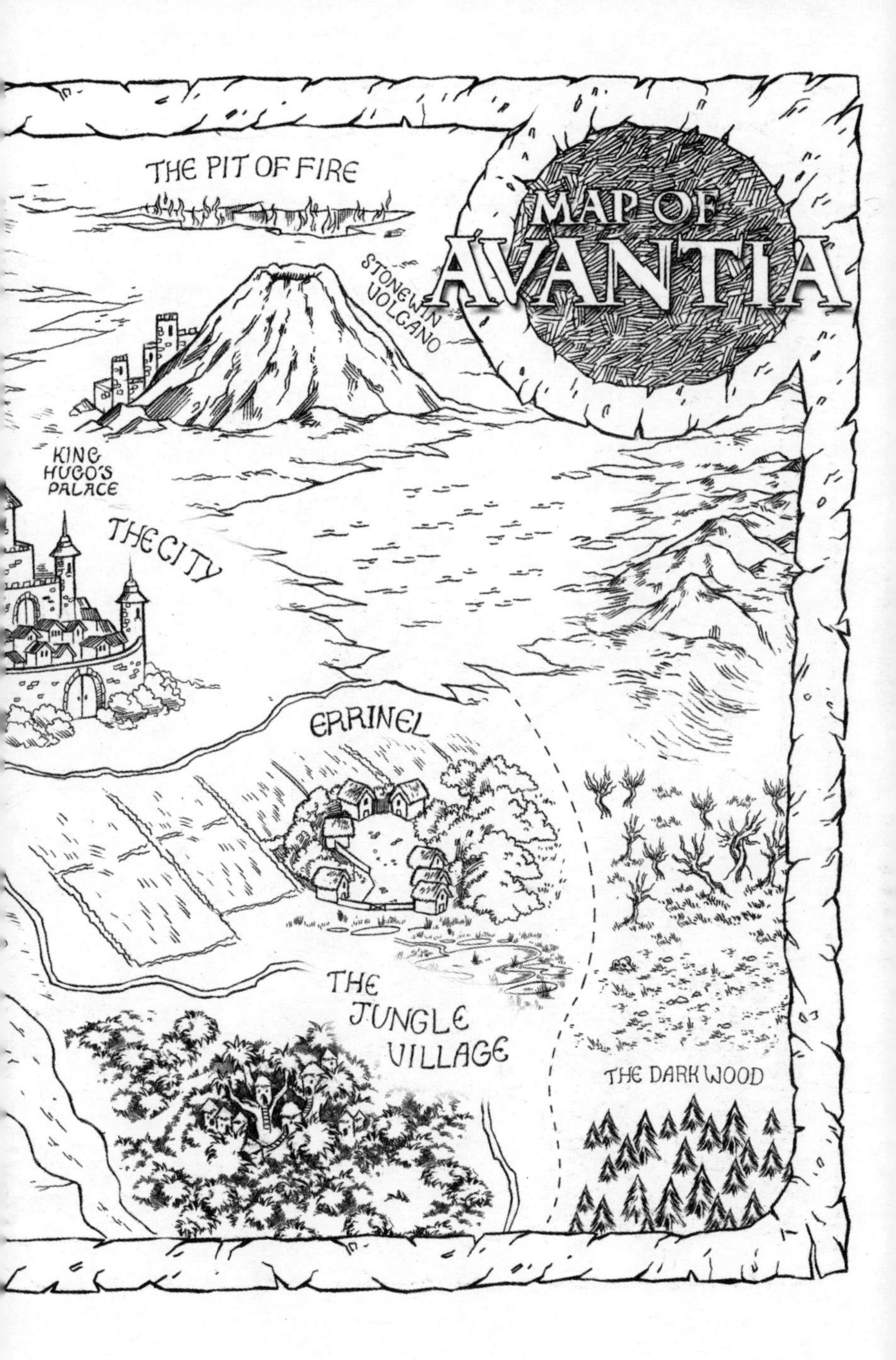
MAP OF
AVANTIA
THE PIT OF FIRE
STONEWIN
VOLCANO
KING
HUGO'S
PALACE
THE CITY
ERRINEL
THE
JUNGLE
VILLAGE
THE DARK WOOD

CONTENTS

I'd forgotten how much I hate this kingdom. The fields full of crops. The clear blue skies. The simple, smiling people, going about their petty lives.

Well, all that is about to change. When I get my hands on the Book of Derthsin, *I will have a whole new world of evil magic at my fingertips.*

King Hugo will pay for his smugness. Avantia will tremble. Its protector Beasts will suffer. But above all, it is Tom who will feel my wrath.

And as he perishes, it will be my smiling face he sees.

It's good to be back!

Malvel

TERRIBLE NEWS

"There it is!" cried Tom, reining in his horse as it crested the hilltop. In the distance, the City glimmered against the evening sky, lit by a hundred torches that flickered from the battlements.

A murmur of relief ran around the royal retinue. The soldiers were slumped wearily over their saddles and many nursed wounds. It had been over a day's hard ride from the Ruby Desert, where Tarantix the Bone Spider had attacked the royal party on its way back from Tangala.

"At last!" gasped King Hugo, embracing Queen Aroha tightly. They were both mounted on a single horse, their royal clothes tattered and streaked with dust.

"We're not there yet," the queen replied. She slapped the horse's rump and it bolted down the hillside towards the City, hooves thundering.

Tom grinned. The queen's baby was waiting for them back in the palace, carried to safety by Elenna when Tarantix had attacked.

"Let's go!" Tom cried, his body filled with a fresh energy.

The sky was almost black as they reached the palace walls. Standing just above the gate was the familiar figure of Captain Harkman, torchlight glinting off his helmet. "Lower the drawbridge!" the captain shouted.

At once it swung down. King Hugo and Queen Aroha went first, followed closely by Tom and the soldiers. Tom felt a warm rush of relief to be back at the palace.

In the centre of the courtyard stood Elenna, awkwardly holding a baby bundled to her chest. Queen Aroha swung herself from the

saddle and rushed to take the child.

"Thank you!" she said, tears coming to her eyes.

King Hugo clapped Elenna on the

back. "How can we ever thank you? You saved our son!"

Elenna caught Tom's eye, and winked. "It wasn't just me," she said. "We all did our bit. I'm just glad he's safe – and you are too!"

"That reminds me," said Hugo, turning to look at the injured soldiers clambering down from their horses. "Get these men to the healers at once!"

As Captain Harkman's soldiers took away the wounded, Tom dismounted and watched the king and queen's happy reunion with their son. He knew he had done the right thing by escorting them back to the palace, but even so he felt uneasy. *They're safe now, but for how long?* Malvel had a head start, and he would surely be using the *Book of Derthsin* to summon another Beast from the Netherworld. *I need to return to my Quest!*

"Are you thinking what I'm thinking?" asked Elenna, as she came to Tom's side. "We need to get after the Dark Wizard, and quickly!"

Tom nodded. "Where's Storm?"

"He's being fed and watered," Elenna said. "I'll show you."

As the two of them set off towards the stable, Daltec stepped out of an archway. The gangly young wizard raised a robed arm in greeting. "Tom!" he said. "What a relief to see you safe and sound!"

A girl appeared behind him, dressed in red, with short dark hair and delicate butterfly wings fluttering at her back. It was Lyra, the Henkrallian witch. She was helping a hunched figure shuffle towards them, as he leaned heavily on a walking stick.

Tom gasped. "I can't believe it!"

Aduro's wrinkled face was almost as white as his beard, but the twinkle was back in his eyes.

"You're better!" Tom cried. Malvel had cast a spell on the former wizard, sending him into a magical sleep.

"I'm not quite my old self yet,"

Aduro admitted. "But I couldn't miss the chance to greet you two heroes!"

Tom and Elenna wrapped the old man up in a hug.

"I don't know what we'd do without you," said Elenna, as they broke apart.

"It's all thanks to Daltec and Lyra," said Aduro. "They saved my life."

"I'm not sure I'd go that far," said Daltec, blushing. But he was grinning proudly all the same.

"We were only too happy to help," added Lyra.

"I wish we could stay," said Tom. "But we have to stop Malvel. He might have already summoned up another Beast."

"Don't be so hasty, Tom," said Aduro. His face had turned grave.

"Is something wrong?" asked Elenna.

"Indeed – all is not as it seems," said Aduro. "The next Beast Malvel summons will be the final one...but I cannot allow you to fight it."

Tom and Elenna looked at each other in shock. "Why not?" asked Tom.

"Because if you were to defeat this creature," said Aduro, "it would destroy Avantia."

1

MALVEL'S PLAN

The candles flickered in Aduro's study, throwing shadows across the books piled high on the desk. Aduro sank down into his carved wooden chair, while Tom, Elenna, Daltec and Lyra stood waiting for him to catch his breath. The wizard had been in a rush to lead them here.

"Pay close attention, all of you,"

said Aduro at last. "What I am about to tell you could sow the seeds of panic, were it to leave this room. But you must understand the truth about the *Book of Derthsin*."

"It's a book of ancient and evil sorcery," said Elenna. "What more do we need to know?"

Aduro stroked his beard, frowning. "I'm afraid it is rather more than that. You see, the Book was buried with Tanner, the first Master of the Beasts, for hundreds of years. During all that time, no one knew what it contained. But before that, the wizard Rufus read it, and copied out several pages by hand. I have one of them here..."

The old man opened a drawer in his desk and pulled out an ancient, yellowed scroll. He spread it out on the desk, and pointed to a map drawn in red ink on the parchment.

At first Tom didn't understand what he was looking at. In the middle of the map a huge chasm was drawn, stretching across most of the parchment. From the hole in the ground, Beasts were pouring out and rampaging across the land.

"Where is this?" asked Tom. Then he saw four red symbols drawn in each corner of the map. Each symbol was a tall column with an image of a Beastly face at the top of it. Tom recognised them straight away. *Those*

are the columns that appeared when we defeated the first three Beasts!

His blood ran cold. "Wait…" he said. "Is this a map of Avantia?"

Aduro nodded and ran his finger over the parchment, following a line of script that ran beneath the map. "*By the blood of four*," he read out loud, "*countless Beasts shall rise, to fill the world with blood and darken the skies*."

"What does it mean?" asked Tom, though he almost didn't want to hear the answer.

"It means the three Beasts Malvel has already conjured are just the beginning," said Aduro. "If you defeat the fourth and final Beast, the fourth column will rise and the magic will be completed. A gateway will open up between Avantia and the Netherworld, and our kingdom will be laid to waste."

The truth hit Tom like a stallion's kick and his hands clenched into fists. *Malvel's tricked us!* And he had fallen for it, right from the start. The Dark Wizard had wanted him to vanquish the Beasts. Each one he defeated had only brought the kingdom one step closer to ruin.

Anger surged through his body as he thought of the shadow paths stretching out from the base of each column. He and Elenna had thought the shadows were there to guide them, but in truth they were there to guide Malvel to where he needed to be to summon the next Beast.

"So we can't defeat the final Beast,"

said Elenna, frowning. "But we can't leave it free to attack Avantia either! So what do we do?"

Tom racked his brains, but there was no solution. *Unless, somehow...* "Could we send the Beast back into the Netherworld?" he asked. "That way it would stay undefeated, and Malvel couldn't open up the gateway."

Aduro leaned forward, narrowing his eyes. "Perhaps," he murmured. "But to do such a thing would take powerful magic indeed. Powerful and dangerous. With my assistance, Daltec could concoct a potion to open a gateway for a little while. Just enough time for you to push the Beast back through it."

"It might work," said Lyra. "But at what cost? While the portal remains open, other Beasts from the Netherworld could use it to enter Avantia."

"Do we have a choice?" asked Elenna.

No one replied.

Suddenly Aduro jerked back in his chair, clutching his head. His eyes bulged with horror.

Tom knelt at the old man's side, his heart racing. "Aduro? What's wrong?"

Aduro's head lolled on his chest. Then he looked up, staring deep into Tom's eyes. A cruel smile twitched on his lips, and Tom felt an icy shiver run through him.

That's not Aduro...Malvel has taken control of him!

"Are you afraid, Tom?" asked Aduro. His voice sounded strange – younger and deeper. It was the voice of the Dark Wizard, coming from Aduro's mouth.

"Get out of him, Malvel!" shouted Elenna. "Leave him alone!"

Aduro's corrupted form laughed harshly. "I've no interest in this old man, I can assure you. He will be dead soon, just like every other Avantian. But you and Tom had better hurry if you wish to defeat my final Beast."

"It's no use, Malvel," said Tom. "We know your plan. If we defeat your Beast, we'll be opening up a gateway to the Netherworld."

"Oh, but I think you will defeat it," the Dark Wizard chuckled through Aduro's lips. "Unless you want to bring mortal peril on your loved ones. You see, Lypida is heading for Errinel right now, Tom. Are you going to sit back and watch while your little village is destroyed, your aunt and uncle slaughtered along with all your oldest friends? I thought you were supposed to be a hero!"

There was another horrible cackle. Then Aduro slumped in his chair, unconscious.

IN PURSUIT

"Aduro?" said Daltec. "Can you hear me, master?"

Lyra knelt and took the old man's hand. For a long moment Aduro was still and silent. Then at last he stirred. When he opened his eyes, Tom could see that Malvel was gone.

"What happened?" croaked Aduro.

"Malvel took control of you," said

Tom, grimly. "But don't worry, we're going to make him pay. We're going to Errinel, right now."

"What about the potion?" said Elenna. "We'll need that if we're to banish this Lypida back to the Netherworld."

"The potion," said Aduro, heaving himself upright. "Of course... But it will take time, I fear."

"We'll make it together," said Daltec, firmly. "And when it's ready, I'll bring it to Tom and Elenna myself."

"Agreed," said Elenna. "In the meantime, we'll keep the Beast busy!"

"I don't like this," said Lyra,

frowning. "To take control of poor Aduro like that – Malvel seems even more powerful than before."

"No doubt he is," said Aduro. "Thanks to the *Book of Derthsin*. Its ancient magic is still deadly potent. You must take great care, both of you."

Tom nodded. "Don't worry, Aduro. I'll defend Errinel – and all of Avantia too!"

Soon afterwards, Tom and Elenna stepped into the darkness of the stables. Storm let out a whinny at the sight of them, and Tom rushed forward to stroke the stallion's mane. "Good to see you too, boy." Then they clambered up into the saddle.

Storm ambled out into the courtyard and flexed the huge feathered wings that Lyra had conjured up for him.

Then he shot forward, jolting Tom and Elenna back in the saddle as his hooves pounded the cobbles. The next moment he launched himself into the air, over the top of the palace wall, up into the night sky.

They wheeled once over the palace, and Tom caught sight of Daltec and Lyra standing on a turret below, waving at them. *I won't let you down*, he thought.

All the same, he couldn't help imagining what would happen if the gateway opened, and Beasts from the Netherworld were let loose to rampage through the kingdom...

He shuddered as Storm flew

through the darkness, leaving the palace behind.

They travelled east, with no light but the glimmering of the stars and the soft glow of the moon, silvering the countryside below. Tom's limbs felt weary from his Quest, but he couldn't stop to rest now – not while his village was in danger.

At last they saw an orange glow on the horizon.

"That's Errinel," said Tom.

"And from that torchlight, it looks like the villagers are awake," said Elenna.

As they flew closer, Tom saw the familiar thatched roofs and the little village square bathed in light.

People were scurrying between the houses, carrying flaming torches and makeshift weapons and shouting to one another.

Tom felt a dull sickness. Some of the houses had collapsed into heaps of rubble. *Collapsed – or been destroyed by something...?*

At a twitch of the reins, Storm flew lower, descending towards the village square.

Something went whistling past Tom's ear.

"They're throwing things at us!" gasped Elenna.

A shout came from below. "Stop that! Can't you see, it's no Beast – it's Tom!"

In spite of the danger, Tom couldn't help grinning at the sound of that voice. *Uncle Henry!*

Storm landed with a soft thump of

hooves on hardened earth. Tom and Elenna swung themselves from the saddle as the familiar figure of Uncle Henry strode over from the shadows by the houses, carrying a torch. Tom's uncle wrapped him up in a hug, then his grin fell, and he looked deadly serious.

"What's going on, Uncle?" asked Tom.

"I wish we knew," said Henry. "Some kind of creature is attacking the village. It's up there in the sky somewhere." He gestured with his torch.

Elenna frowned. "We didn't see anything."

"That's because it's as dark and

silent as a shadow," said Henry. "We've been trying to fight back, but we keep losing track of it."

"Then you'd better get inside," said Tom. A crowd was gathering around them, and Tom spoke up to address them all. "Please! Get to safety! We'll handle this."

"We're not going to hide," shouted a young girl, fiercely, from across the square. Tom realised it was Lily, the daughter of the village cobbler. She'd always been fierce and brave. She clutched a flaming torch in one hand, and her father's mallet in the other. "We'll defend our homes," she cried. "To the death, if we have to!"

Tom felt a flicker of pride at the

bravery of his fellow villager. Then a gust of wind swept through the square, making the torches gutter.

Craning his neck, Tom looked up and gasped. A huge, dark shape was swooping overhead, diving towards Lily. She stood her ground, the flames of torch lighting up the look of grim determination on her face.

Tom darted forward, fighting through the crowd to get to her. "Get down!" he shouted, but Lily drew back her arm to swing the mallet. A moment later, Tom barrelled into her, knocking her down. The torch went rolling away, still burning. A gust of foul wind swept over Tom as the giant creature passed above, so close he could almost feel the rustling of its wings. *What is that thing?*

Glancing up, Tom saw the Beast banking away from the square. It was lit clearly now in the glow of torches, and what Tom saw made his breath freeze in his chest.

The Beast was a gigantic moth, with mottled, brownish wings that shimmered in the darkness. The wings were tipped with savage-looking metallic hooks.

"I've always wanted to fight a Beast!" said Lily. Then her eyes widened. "It's coming back!"

Tom rolled away from her and got to his feet.

"Why aren't you drawing your

sword?" asked Lily.

Tom shook his head. "I can't kill this Beast."

The girl stared at him. "What do you mean?"

Before Tom could reply, the Beast came curving round and dived at an elderly man, fast as lightning. A whip-like, barbed tentacle lashed out from the moth's body, curled around the man's waist and heaved him up into the air. The villager kicked and struggled, shouting out in terror. Hiss companions rushed to grab hold of his legs, but they were simply lifted up with him, all dangling from the Beast's powerful tentacle. In a moment they would all be carried into the night sky...

Tom was too far away. *I can't get there in time!* He looked around, then crawled to Lily's fallen torch. Picking it up, he threw it at the Beast as hard as he could. The torch spun through the air, blazing end over end, and struck the giant moth's body with a shower of sparks.

Screeeeeeeeee! Tom clapped his hands over his ears as the Beast let out a terrible shriek of rage. Most of the villagers flinched at the deafening sound, cowering in horror. The tentacle whipped away, dropping the men in a heap on the ground. The Beast flapped her wings, and swooped towards Tom.

Tom tried to dive out of the way but the enormous moth was too fast, and her body was hard to track against the night sky. *Thud!* Her wing struck him hard, knocking him off his feet. The back of his head smashed against the ground. Pain throbbed through his temples.

"Hey! Come and get me!" It was Elenna's voice. Tom saw her waving

her torch in the sky, running away from the crowd of villagers. Another gust of wind surged through the square as the moth came gliding down towards her. She stopped in the middle of the square and turned to face the Beast.

"Run!" shouted Tom, but Elenna stood her ground, watching as the Beast loomed closer and closer. Any second now, the moth would sink those savage hooks into her...

MOTH TO A FLAME

Elenna spun on her heel and tossed the flaming torch in an arc of light. There was splash and a hiss, and the flame was gone. Tom realised it must have struck the millpond and sunk underwater.

Screeeee! With a mighty flap of her wings, Lypida surged back into the sky, as though she had lost interest in Elenna entirely.

"It's the flames!" called Elenna triumphantly. "The Beast is attracted to them. That's why she's attacking – because of the bright lights!" She turned to the villagers. "All of you, put your torches out!"

The villagers exchanged nervous glances, but Uncle Henry nodded, put his own torch on the ground and stamped out the flames. One by one, his companions did the same. The light died away in the village square, leaving them finally in darkness.

For a while they waited, everyone rooted to the spot, waiting for the telltale screech of the giant moth… but there was nothing. Lypida had vanished into the night.

Tom let out a sigh of relief. "Great thinking, Elenna," he said. "The village is safe for now."

"Thanks to you two," said Aunt Maria. Uncle Henry's wife emerged from the crowd and joined hands with Henry. "But this isn't like you, Tom. Why didn't you face the Beast?"

Tom looked round the darkened square and saw that all the assembled villagers were staring at him, waiting to hear his answer. He shook his head. "I wish I could, but it's complicated. This Beast is from another realm. I can't defeat her, but I can send her back there. And that's what I'm going to do."

As the villagers muttered to each other in puzzlement, Tom motioned to Elenna. Together they clambered up on to Storm's back. The stallion tossed his head, then reared up, taking off with a single beat of his feathered wings.

They weaved between thick grey clouds, following the direction in which Lypida had flown off. Tom kept looking all around, but he couldn't see any sign of the giant moth. *Have we lost her?* Once or twice he reached for his belt, his fingers brushing over the red jewel of Torgor to see if he could detect the Beast's thoughts from up ahead – but there was nothing.

"She can't be too far ahead," muttered Elenna. "We'll catch up with her soon."

As she spoke, Tom saw something in the distance – a great patch of darkness sprawling across the land – and his heart quickened. *The*

Dark Wood... A terrifying forest in the Forbidden Land, where Tom and Elenna had gone on a Quest from which they almost didn't return.

Tom stroked Storm's neck, and his stallion climbed higher in the sky. *If we can lure the Beast into the trees, she won't be able to swoop down on us from above!*

On the eastern horizon, Tom saw that the sky was lightening, turning deep blue as the dawn approached.

"A new day in Avantia," said Elenna. "That's if we can stop Malvel from opening up the gateway to the Netherworld."

Suddenly Tom heard Storm let out a panicked snort.

"What's wrong, boy?" asked Tom. Then he caught sight of something, and his heart lurched. At the tips of Storm's wings, the feathers were fluttering away. The stallion beat his wings harder, but more feathers fell with every stroke.

In horror, Tom remembered the words of Lyra, when she had enchanted Storm and given him the power of flight. *My spell won't last for ever…*

"He's losing his wings!" said Elenna. "We've got to get down lower."

But it was too late – the feathers were falling in great clumps now. Tom felt Storm falter and lurch

downwards. The stallion whinnied again, and spread his wings, but they were dropping fast.

Tom scoured the treetops of the forest, desperately searching for a place to land. Something glimmered with moonlight in a clearing – a lake of still water.

"There!" he shouted, pointing. "Can you make it, Storm?"

The stallion flapped his wings valiantly, but Tom could feel the wind rushing through his hair and buffeting his face as they plummeted faster and faster towards the forest.

THE END OF YOUR WORLD

Storm gave one last beat of his wings, carrying them a fraction higher over the treetops. Then down they went, trailing feathers.

SPLASH!

Tom's body was gripped with icy cold, and for an instant all sound was muffled. He sank in a flurry of bubbles, before surfacing through a crash of spray.

Rubbing the water from his eyes, Tom saw Storm surge out of the lake not far away, flicking water from his mane.

"You did it, boy!" called Tom, and the stallion whinnied in reply.

It was a short swim to the bank, and soon Tom and Elenna were wading on to dry land, their clothes sodden. Storm trotted over wearily. His wings had gone completely, leaving him just as he was before Lyra's spell.

"Storm has done us proud," said Elenna, wringing out her hair. "But we can't fly any further now."

Tom nodded. "But maybe we don't need to. We're close to the Dark Wood – we can ride the rest of– "

Whhhhhsshhh!

A tentacle came lashing down from the night sky, and Tom gasped as hot

pain lanced through his back. He fell to his knees. His back was burning. He reached for the wound and felt a rip in his tunic. When he looked at his fingers there was blood on them.

Glancing up, he saw Lypida disappearing into the night, tentacle trailing. Elenna was already fitting an arrow to her bowstring.

"No," said Tom, gritting his teeth against the pain. "We can't kill the Beast, remember?"

Elenna frowned fiercely, but she lowered her bow.

A great shadow fell across them again, and Tom saw the giant moth soaring out above the treetops, her tentacle trailing like a fisherman's line searching for a catch.

"We should get in among the trees," said Elenna.

Tom looked around, wincing at the stinging of his wound. Then he shook his head. "As long as Lypida can fly, she's got the advantage over us. But if we could get her wings wet..."

"The lake!" said Elenna. "Good idea, Tom. So how do we– "

Screeeee! Lypida came swooping down. Her tendril swung, the point glinting in the moonlight. But instead of dodging, Tom reached up and caught it, clinging on with all his strength. It felt like thick rope in his hands, damp and rough, but he swallowed his horror and tugged

downwards, trying to keep the moth from flying away.

"Hang on, Tom!" called Elenna.

Lypida let out another terrible screech. She flapped her wings, sending gusts of wind that broke

off branches from the surrounding trees and made Tom's eyes water. But he drew on the power of the golden breastplate, and felt magical strength surge through his arms. Little by little, he began to tug the Beast towards the edge of the moonlit lake.

Just a little further...

Suddenly the Beast twisted and flapped hard, as though she had understood what Tom was planning. He gripped as hard as he could, but the Beast was stronger. With a flick of her tendril, she squirmed free and shot up into the sky. Tom sprawled on the ground, his palms burning. *No!* He watched as the giant moth climbed upwards, a dark shadow getting further and further away.

"She'll be back," said Elenna.

But instead, Lypida wheeled in the sky and flew away over the forest.

Tom frowned as he clambered to

his feet. *Why is she fleeing?* Then he saw something in the distance. A white light hanging low over the treetops like the moon, but so bright it made him squint to look directly at it.

"That's where she's going," said Elenna. "She's attracted to light, remember?" Sure enough, the Beast was a black dot silhouetted against the light.

An uneasy feeling swirled in Tom's gut. "I don't like this," he muttered. "Let's get after her."

Tom and Elenna climbed up on to Storm's back, and the stallion set off, galloping through the shadows among the trees.

Tom soon lost sight of Lypida, but they kept going in the same direction, following glimpses of the strange light seen through the branches.

Finally they rode out into a clearing that was bathed in a white glow. Up above, a strange orb hovered, looking like a shining crystal ball that was luminous with magic.

"There!" said Elenna, and Tom saw Lypida fluttering through the gradually lightening sky of dawn, flying in circles around the orb.

Then Tom saw something else that made him tense all over, sending pain stinging through his wounded back. Crouched on the branch of a tree, at the edge of the clearing, was a man in a green robe. The hood was drawn up so that Tom couldn't see his face. But there was no doubt who it was.

Malvel!

The Dark Wizard pointed his staff up at the orb, and the tip of it glowed with the same white light. *He's made the orb using his magic! But why?*

Lypida let out a sudden shriek. Jerking his gaze upwards, Tom saw that the Beast must have touched the orb with one of her wings. Now the orb was transforming, splitting into a glowing network of strands which engulfed the giant moth like a spider's web. Lypida's wings twitched, but they were held fast. The Beast fell, thumping down on to the ground in the middle of the clearing. She lay there, squirming helplessly, wrapped up in a net of pure white light.

Tom and Elenna dismounted and raced forward. But before they could reach the Beast, Malvel dropped from the tree, landing in a crouch. He flicked out his staff, and at once a wall of magical fire sprang up, stretching across the clearing in front of Lypida. *Whumph!* Tom and Elenna came skidding to a halt, the heat of the fire warming their faces.

As the flames crackled, Malvel stood and stepped forward. A savage smile curved his lips. "I was wondering when you two would show up. Just a little too late, I'm afraid! This stupid Beast was all too easy to trick. Now all that's left is for me to slay her, and the fourth column will rise. And you know what that means, don't you, Tom?"

Tom's gaze flicked from side to side, but the fire burned hot and bright, the flames licking up as tall as Malvel. There was no way through.

"Don't do it," shouted Elenna. "You'll regret it, Malvel. Do you really think you can control the Beasts of the Netherworld?"

Malvel chuckled. "Actually, with the *Book of Derthsin*, I can. Its magic is powerful indeed. Didn't that old fool Aduro tell you that? "

The Dark Wizard raised his staff, and in a flash the end of it transformed into a curved blade. The metal shone like a mirror in the white glow of the net.

Malvel crossed the clearing to where Lypida lay. He raised the bladed staff, and smiled at Tom. Firelight danced in his eyes, a gaze of pure triumph.

"Are you ready, Tom?" he asked. "Are you ready for the end of your world?"

WINGS OF TERROR

Not while there's blood in my veins!

Tom closed his eyes, feeling the scorching heat of the fire as he drew a deep breath. Then he ran forward and launched himself into the air.

Heat seared through him, the flames licking up all around as he flew through Malvel's wall of fire. Ferno's scale in Tom's shield protected him from the worst of the magical flames. Then his eyes were open and he was stumbling on the other side. Looking down, he saw the edge of his tunic was alight, but there was no time to do anything about it. He hurtled forward, drawing his sword.

Malvel hesitated for just an instant. Then his blade came flashing down towards the Beast's neck.

CLANG!

Tom caught the blow with his own sword, and Malvel's weapon skittered away.

There was a flash of light, and

Tom blinked. When he looked again, he saw that the wizard's blade had passed through the net of light, slicing a gap into it.

Lypida began to squirm once again,

her muscled grey body working at the weakened bonds.

"You fool!" Malvel hissed at Tom. "It's almost as though you want to die!"

Tom beat out the flames on his tunic. Then he crouched down behind his shield, facing Malvel. "I'll happily give my life to save the kingdom."

"Let's make it quick, then," snarled the Dark Wizard. He reached out a hand and his bladed staff flew back into his palm.

Malvel darted forward, the weapon whirling above his head. He sliced again and again, quicker than a striking scorpion. Tom stepped backwards, meeting each blow with his shield. *Thunk! Thunk! Thunk!* He felt the heat of the flames at his back, and his arm shook with the impacts, but he breathed deeply, waiting for a chance to strike. *Stay calm, Tom.*

Malvel paused, watching Tom. The staff rested on his shoulder, ready to swing down at any moment. "Aren't you going to fight back? How disappointing!" Then a nasty sneer spread across his face. "I wonder what your father would say if he could see you now?"

Tom felt his muscles tense at the mention of Taladon.

"Don't let him get to you!"

shouted Elenna, from beyond the wall of fire. She loosed an arrow, but Malvel batted it aside with his staff and it whizzed past, sinking harmlessly into a tree trunk.

"Oh, I forgot!" said Malvel, his gaze still fixed on Tom. "Taladon wouldn't say a thing, would he? Because he's stuck for ever on the Isle of Ghosts. All on his own... because his dear son failed him!"

A hot rush of anger shot through Tom's body. *Don't talk about my father!* Before he could stop himself, he lunged forward, swinging wildly with his sword.

Malvel stepped to one side, and Tom stumbled. He felt a sharp blow to the back of his legs from the butt of Malvel's staff, then toppled on to his knees. He tried to stand, but Malvel thrust the staff again, stabbing the butt into Tom's stomach so hard that he doubled

over, groaning in pain.

As he raised his head, he saw the Dark Wizard looming over him. Beyond, Lypida struggled her way free of the net. *She's almost there... but if Malvel turns around and sees, it's all over!*

"You should give up," said Tom. "Even with the book, you'll never be able to control the Beasts from the Netherworld. You're no great sorcerer, like Derthsin."

Malvel's face clouded with fury, and his fingers tightened on his staff. "That's where you're wrong, Tom. I'm the greatest sorcerer that ever lived!"

"Apart from Aduro," said Tom.

"And Daltec. And Lyra."

"How dare you!" roared Malvel. He raised his staff up high.

Screeee!

The Dark Wizard whirled round at Lypida's cry. The gigantic moth had finally wriggled free, shrugging the last of the net from her great brown wings. In one bound she was airborne, her wings whirring as they carried her up into the deep blue sky.

"You tricked me!" snarled Malvel, turning on Tom.

Tom managed a smile, in spite of the pain in his stomach and across his back. "So now we're even," he said.

Malvel growled and pulled

something from inside his robes – a hefty, ancient tome. *It's the* Book of Derthsin*!* Flicking through, Malvel found a page and began to read out loud. It was a language Tom didn't recognise. But a moment later, he saw Lypida wheel in the sky and return, swooping back towards them.

Malvel's using the book to control her!

Sure enough, Lypida flapped her wings hard as she grew near, each one a thunderclap which sent a rush of wind racing towards Tom.

Staggering to his feet, Tom found himself buffeted back by the gust of wind. The flames of Malvel's firewall surged with each stroke. Then smoke billowed up as the fire was extinguished, like candles snuffed out in King Hugo's palace.

Tom sheathed his sword and darted through the smoke which filled the clearing, coughing. "Elenna!" he shouted. His friend emerged from the grey haze, and they raced to the edge of the clearing, taking shelter with Storm among the trees.

"Lypida can't get to us here," said Elenna.

But as she spoke, the dark shape of the moth loomed overhead, and Lypida flapped her wings one more time.

CRACK!

Looking up, Tom saw a heavy branch break away with the sheer force of Lypida's wing stroke. "Look out!" he cried in terror.

But it was too late. The falling branch struck Elenna on the head with a sickening thud, and she slumped to the ground.

GATEWAY TO THE NETHERWORLD

"Elenna!" gasped Tom, kneeling at her side. He took her shoulders and turned her over, but her eyes were shut. "Can you hear me?"

Nothing...

Then her eyelids flickered, and she smiled. "It'll take more than a bit of wood to stop me," she murmured.

Grinning, Tom helped Elenna to her feet. A bruise was blossoming on her forehead, but apart from that she looked unharmed.

"Tom!" cried a familiar voice.

Turning, Tom saw a young man stumbling through the smoke at the edge of the clearing. *Daltec!*

The wizard spotted them and came closer, coughing. His face was pale and there were bags under his eyes, but he looked determined as he pulled a small glass vial from his sleeve. Inside, a thick black liquid sloshed like oil.

"Is that what I think it is?" asked Elenna.

"It's Aduro's potion," said Daltec.

"It wasn't easy to create, but we did it. Just a few drops will open a gateway to the Netherworld."

A shadowy figure appeared in the smoke behind him.

"Look out!" shouted Tom. Daltec began to turn, but the shadow pounced, one arm curving round Daltec's neck while the other snatched the vial from out of his hand.

"Well, well," hissed Malvel. "I think it's best I take charge of this." A dagger glinted in his hand, hovering close to Daltec's throat.

"Let me go," gasped the young wizard.

Malvel shook his head. "I don't

think so. Not until you tell me what's in this bottle."

He didn't hear what Daltec said!

"Don't tell him!" said Elenna.

Daltec looked terrified, but he said nothing.

Malvel sighed. "I see. Then I'm afraid you're no use to me at all." He twisted the blade, pushing the edge up against Daltec's skin.

Whhhhhsshhh! Tom felt the wind as an arrow shot past him. *Thump!* Malvel dropped the dagger and the vial and stumbled backwards, clutching at his shoulder where a feathered shaft protruded.

Nice shot, Elenna!

Daltec snatched up the vial and

rushed forward, but he tripped on the hem of his robe. As he fell he clawed at the air, and the vial went flying, spinning end over end.

"No!" shouted Tom.

He dived forward, but it was too

late. The vial struck a rock and smashed, spattering black goo. The liquid began to hiss and steam, and where it fell the ground seemed to be collapsing, caving inwards.

Tom backed away. He met Elenna's gaze, just as horrified as his own.

"What have I done...?" moaned Daltec. The poor wizard looked distraught.

The ground kept falling away, as though eaten up by the black liquid. Now there was a chasm wide enough for a man to fit through, but it kept growing, faster and faster, almost filling the clearing. Within, there was nothing but darkness.

"Stay away from the edge," said Daltec. "Don't go near it."

Storm let out a whinny of terror, hooves clopping as he edged away through the trees.

Malvel choked out a laugh, still clutching at the arrow. "Oh, this is better than I could ever have imagined! Now I understand... You fools have opened up a gateway to the Netherworld yourselves!"

As if in answer, a chorus of strange howls rose up from the depths of the pit. *The roars of Beasts!* Tom felt an icy shiver run through him – they sounded like no creature he had ever faced before.

"Soon my Beast army will be

here," said Malvel, his eyes gleaming with triumph.

Daltec scrambled to Tom's side. "It won't stay open for long," he said breathlessly.

"Then we've got no time to lose," said Tom. "We've got to get Lypida

back into the Netherworld, before any of those Beasts escape into Avantia!"

He peered at the lightening sky through the tree branches, but the giant moth was nowhere to be seen.

"We need a bright light," said Elenna desperately.

"Good idea," said Tom. "Daltec, can you conjure some? It will bring the Beast to us."

"Bring the Beast to us?" said Daltec, nervously.

"It's the only way," said Tom.

Daltec hesitated, then he closed his eyes and nodded. Holding out both hands, he began to mutter under his breath.

Shreds of light spilled from his fingertips, circling and coming together in mid-air like a swirling ball of wool. In moments, Daltec had a glowing white orb as big as a cannonball but so bright Tom had to partly shield his eyes. The wizard flung his hands up, tossing it into the air. It soared up above the treetops, glowing like a little moon.

For a moment the orb just hovered there. Then there was a rustle of wings, and with a leap of his heart Tom saw the shadowy form of

Lypida circling nearby, fluttering towards the light.

"You did it!" breathed Elenna.

The chasm was getting wider and wider, and on the other side of it Malvel waited, peering into it with hungry eyes.

No time to lose!

Tom darted to the nearest tree and began to climb, feet scrabbling at the bark. He hauled himself up into the branches, gaze fixed on the orb of light which hovered just above the treetop.

If I can just grab Lypida's tentacle...

Tom pulled himself up to the highest branch and stood, balancing carefully. Above the canopy, he could see the forest spread out all around and feel the breeze on his face, buffeting him and forcing him to crouch down.

Lypida flew closer, her tendril dangling. *Close enough...* But if he timed it wrong, Tom knew that the savage point would cut him to ribbons. And with him dead, the Beasts of the Netherworld would be free to run riot through Avantia...

Taking a deep breath, he launched himself into the air, reaching out. His hands closed on the tentacle, and he gripped hard. He swung in mid-air, as Lypida let out a furious cry.

The giant moth flapped upwards,

tentacle flailing as she tried to throw Tom off. But Tom clung on with all his strength.

Lypida banked and swooped low over the forest, dragging Tom through whipping branches and leaves. *She's trying to knock me off!*

Tensing his muscles, Tom heaved himself up, climbing the tentacle like a rope. He reached up to take hold of the Beast's wings, then swung himself on to Lypida's back, lying flat against the smooth, cool surface of the Beast's body.

Lypida flapped more desperately than ever, but Tom stayed perfectly still. Right in the middle of the giant moth's back, there was no way she

could reach him.

Glancing down, Tom saw that the Beast had circled back and was soaring towards the clearing where the chasm to the Netherworld gaped open. From above Tom spotted the glinting of a thousand eyes deep inside.

There was no way he could let those creatures into Avantia.

This is my one chance!

Tom drew his sword, gripping the hilt tightly. He waited, ready to strike, until the giant moth was fluttering right above the chasm. Then he brought the flat of his blade down hard on the Beast's right wing.

Thwack!

Lypida's wing went limp at once. She flapped desperately with her one good wing, but it wasn't enough. The next moment she was falling, faster and faster.

Tom gritted his teeth and held on as they dropped down into the gaping entrance to the Netherworld. The chasm raced towards them, like the mouth of a monster coming to swallow Tom and Lypida whole.

INTO THE ABYSS

Tom sheathed his sword, then dropped into a crouch, the wind rushing through his hair. At the last moment he drew on the power of the golden boots. As the magical strength flowed into his legs he leapt, pushing off the Beast's back, his arms reaching for the edge of the chasm.

Crunch! Tom gritted his teeth at the sound of breaking bone, and he winced in pain. His right arm had smacked against a rocky ledge. The fingers of his left hand closed over a jagged piece of stone, and took

the weight of his body. He felt his legs sway as he dangled above the darkness.

With a quick glance below, Tom saw Lypida tumbling deeper and deeper, screeching horribly, until at last she disappeared into the shadowy depths.

He breathed deep, trying to stay calm. His right arm hung limp, definitely broken. He was bruised and battered, and his left hand burned with the pain of holding on. No way to climb up with only one arm. It was only a matter of time before he followed Lypida into the Netherworld.

Then something snaked out from above – a rope unfurling from the edge of the pit. *Rope from Storm's saddlebag!* Relief flooded Tom's body as he saw Elenna's face peering down from above.

"Grab hold of it!" she shouted.

The rope hung right by Tom's hand, but to take it he would have to let go for an instant. *Here goes...* As he released his fingers his body started to drop, but he shoved off the rockface with his feet and hurled himself towards the rope. As his fingers closed he clung on tight, spinning and bashing again against the vertical wall. Pain lanced up his injured arm, and he almost lost consciousness. A moment later, he felt himself rising.

A snuffling, growling sound made Tom look back over his shoulder. He caught his breath. He could see shadowy shapes emerging from the darkness below. They were Beasts, climbing up the walls of the chasm. Moonlight fell on them, glinting off savage glaring eyes, curved talons, horns and worse still. With a shiver, Tom remembered the words from the *Book of Derthsin*: "Countless Beasts shall rise, to fill the world with blood and darken the skies."

They're coming to attack Avantia!

"Nearly there!" called Elenna from above. Tom looked up, and realised in horror that the chasm was shrinking, the edges already beginning to knit back together. But the next moment Tom found himself heaved up on to the edge of the pit, where he collapsed, panting. "Thank you," he gasped out to Elenna and Daltec, who clutched the other end of the rope.

Elenna shook her head. "Don't mention—"

WHOOOSH! A bolt of green light struck her in the chest, lifting her off her feet and knocking her to the ground.

Tom scrambled up as a second bolt shot past. It smacked into Daltec, leaving him in a heap on the ground.

Whirling round, Tom raised his shield to meet a third bolt. *THUMP!* His good arm jarred with the impact,

the shield shuddering as green light spilled round the sides.

When he lowered it, Tom saw Malvel striding towards them around the edge of the shrinking chasm, his staff levelled in one hand. Its bladed tip was glowing green.

"What have you done to them?" shouted Tom.

"Oh, nothing they won't recover from," sneered Malvel. "I'd hate for them to miss the end of the world. You, on the other hand... I think I'll just send you to join your father now. You've been a thorn in my side for long enough, Tom."

Malvel drew his staff back like a spear, as he broke into a run.

Tom's heart was thumping as he settled into a fighting crouch. He had his shield, but his sword arm was useless, dangling broken at his side. *But Malvel's no better off!* Elenna's arrow still stuck out from the Dark Wizard's shoulder, and his left hand was wrapped around the shaft. *Looks like we're both fighting one-handed.*

With a grunt, Malvel lunged. Tom knocked the blow aside with his shield, metal scraping on wood. He lashed out with a foot, trying to kick his opponent in the chest. But instead Malvel swung his staff and struck Tom on the shin, making him stumble. "It's only a matter of time, Tom," Malvel taunted. "You can't hurt me with a shield, can you?"

As Malvel raised his staff for a final blow, Tom shook his head. "No..." *But I can break that staff!*

Malvel swung, and Tom sidestepped. The blade scythed

down and sank deep into the soft soil of the forest floor. And before Malvel could tug it free, Tom drove the edge of his shield down like an axe, smashing through the middle of the staff.

Crack! The wood shattered with an eerie green glow.

Malvel's face twisted with a rage as savage as any Tom had ever seen. He tossed the broken end of his staff into the chasm, which had shrunk to twenty paces across. "You think that will stop me?" he shrieked. "I have the *Book of Derthsin*!"

Backing away, Malvel drew the ancient tome from his robes and flipped it open. "The magic in here will keep the gateway open, Tom, you'll see!" He began to read, muttering fast under his breath.

Tom strode towards him, anger surging through his body. "I don't think so, Malvel," he said. "And

I've had enough of your ranting!"
Darting forward, he launched a kick at the book. His foot connected hard with the thick volume.

The *Book of Derthsin* flew through the air, straight towards the chasm. Malvel let out a strangled squawk and dived, clutching at it. His hands closed on the book.

For an instant, Tom's eyes met those of the Dark Wizard, and he could see nothing there but fear. Then Malvel's weight carried him over the edge and he fell like a boulder into the Netherworld, his robes streaming behind him, still clutching on to the *Book of Derthsin*.

Tom rushed to the edge of the hole,

which continued to grow smaller
by the moment, but Malvel had
already disappeared into the depths,

somewhere among the glittering eyes and teeth of the Beasts below. All that remained was the echo of his terrified cry.

The ground rumbled. Tom stepped back as the ground closed on itself like a snapping mouth. The last of the rumbling died away, and then there was nothing but an empty clearing and the sounds of the dawn forest.

Tom sank to his knees, panting. All at once, exhaustion had flooded his body.

A short distance away, Elenna stirred and propped herself up on her elbows. Beside her, Daltec was rolling over, groaning. Elenna blinked blearily at Tom, looking as though she had just woken from a very long sleep. "What happened?" she croaked. "What did I miss?"

Tom grinned. "Only the end of the world," he said.

Tom had never felt so glad to be back at the palace, in the cosy warmth of Aduro's study. While Aduro, Daltec and Lyra stood talking with Captain Harkman by the window, he and Elenna relaxed in a pair of cushioned chairs.

"There's one thing I don't understand," said Elenna, pointing to Tom's right arm. "Why don't you just heal it? You've got the magic of the

green jewel, remember!"

Tom looked down at his broken arm, wrapped up in a white linen sling. He shrugged and smiled. "I suppose I've had enough of magic for a while." He lowered his voice to a whisper. "Besides...this gives me the perfect excuse for a little rest!"

"You've earned it," said Aduro, making Tom jump. *I can't believe how good his hearing is!*

The old man settled into his own chair behind his desk. "You've defeated Malvel once again."

"But is he really gone?" asked Captain Harkman, gravely.

"He's returned before," said Lyra.

"Even from the Isle of Ghosts," added Daltec.

Aduro shook his head firmly. "This is different. No one could survive for long in the Netherworld. It's not an end I would wish on anyone, even a man so twisted as Malvel. Yes, I believe this is the end of him."

Tom could have sworn he saw a moment of doubt flicker across Aduro's features. But before he could ask any questions, the door swung open with a creak.

Turning in his seat, Tom saw King Hugo and Queen Aroha standing in the doorway. The queen held her baby swaddled in her arms.

Daltec, Lyra and Captain Harkman all dropped to their knees, but King Hugo waved, motioning for them to stand. "Please!" he said. "It's we who should be kneeling to you. You risked your lives to save our kingdom.

Especially you, Tom and Elenna."

"We came to thank you," said Queen Aroha. "And to tell you that we have chosen a name for our son, at last."

The royal couple exchanged a glance. "You should tell him," said King Hugo.

Queen Aroha smiled and shook her head.

"Very well, then," said King Hugo. "The heir to the royal thrones of Avantia and Tangala will be called... Prince Thomas. We named him after the bravest hero in the land."

Tom felt his cheeks flushing bright red as Elenna turned to grin at him. "Well, go on then!" she said, jabbing him in the ribs. "Say something!"

"It's an honour," said Tom. "I'm just proud to serve my king and queen." He looked round at the room of smiling faces, and smiled back.

The Quest was over, but Tom had a feeling it wouldn't be his last.

THE END

DANGER
1

CONGRATULATIONS, YOU HAVE COMPLETED THIS QUEST!

At the end of each chapter you were
awarded a special gold coin.
The QUEST in this book was
worth an amazing 8 coins.

Look at the Beast Quest totem picture inside the back cover of this book to see how far you've come in your journey to become

MASTER OF THE BEASTS.

The more books you read,
the more coins you will collect!

Do you want your own
Beast Quest Totem?

1. Cut out and collect the coin below
2. Go to the Beast Quest website
3. Download and print out your totem
4. Add your coin to the totem

www.beastquest.co.uk/totem

8

Don't miss the first exciting Beast Quest book in this series, GRYMON THE BITING HORROR!

Read on for a sneak peek...

THE BROKEN TOMB

A bead of sweat dripped from Elenna's brow. Her knuckles were white on the hilt of her sword. Tom circled, looking for an opening. She crossed her feet, and he pounced, bringing his own blade down. She blocked, and tripped, landing hard on her behind. Tom pointed the tip of his wooden sword at her neck. "Got

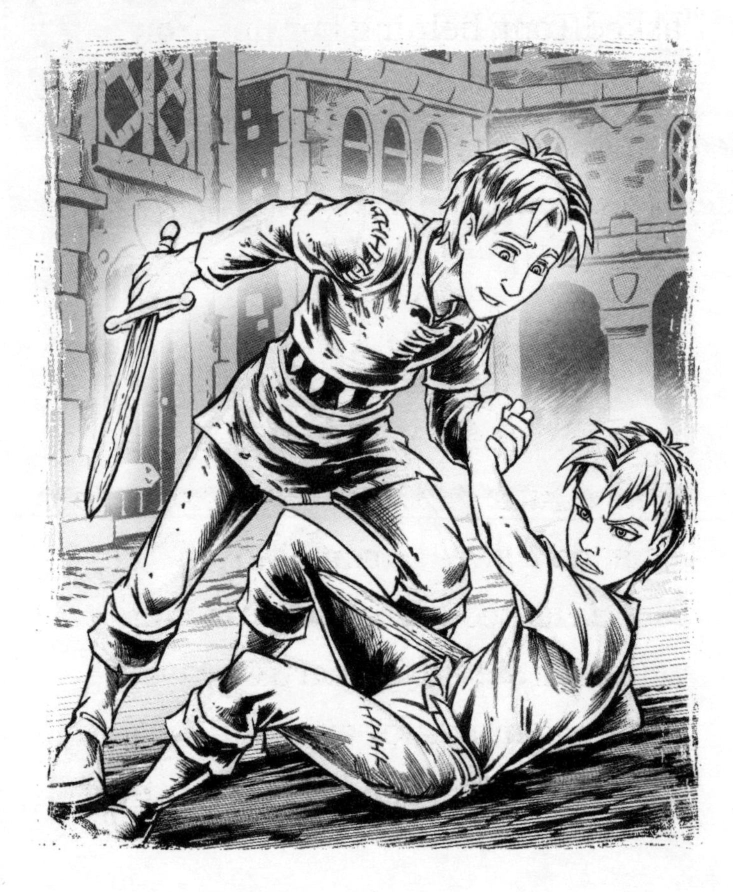

you again!"

Elenna growled, clearly annoyed at her mistake.

"What's wrong with you today?" asked Tom, helping her up. "You should never cross your feet in a duel – that's basic footwork."

"I know that," said Elenna, dusting herself off. "I suppose my mind is elsewhere."

Tom nodded grimly. It wasn't easy to forget the peril Avantia faced. Their Quest to the Isle of Ghosts had been a success in some ways – they had defeated several Beasts and returned safely. But in other ways, the danger was greater than ever. For they'd brought back with them an old enemy who Tom had thought was gone for ever – the evil sorcerer, Malvel.

"I can't help wondering where he is," muttered Elenna. "When he's going to strike."

Tom squared his shoulders. "And that's why we must keep practising," he said. "So we're ready."

The two companions were training in the courtyard of King Hugo's palace, as they had every day since they'd returned. And each day, Tom expected to hear news of some chaos breaking out in the kingdom. Malvel had returned from the dead, his evil spirit inhabiting the body of the wayward young wizard, Berric.

The thought that their great enemy had risen from the grave to threaten Avantia once again was almost too much for Tom to bear.

A fanfare of trumpets sounded from the castle battlements. A voice rang out. "Open the gates for Captain Harkman!"

Tom turned, heart thumping, as the huge gates were drawn open.

Captain Harkman rode in on his great black charger, a plumed helmet on his head, his breastplate gleaming, his long red cloak spread over his horse's rump. The captain commanded the regular search parties sent out to scour the land for any trace of Malvel.

Tom and Elenna ran forward to greet him as he swung down from the saddle. The grizzle-haired old warrior removed his helmet and saluted them solemnly.

"Is there any news?" Tom asked, searching the captain's face.

Harkman shook his head. "Not even a trace. My men have scoured the kingdom from border to border. We've questioned countless villagers. No one has seen any sign of Berric, or Malvel." He sighed, then added hopefully, "Perhaps he has fled Avantia for good."

Tom frowned. "It's possible, I suppose, but Malvel hates this kingdom more than anything. And he's a master sorcerer. If we haven't found him, it's probably because he doesn't want to be found."

Captain Harkman nodded. "I must carry my reports to Daltec."

"We'll come with you," said Elenna.

They followed the gruff captain into the palace, guards coming to attention as they strode past.

The heavy doors to the throne room swung wide and they made their way down the long aisle to where the royal throne stood under the banners and flags of Avantia.

The throne was empty, of course. King Hugo had taken his pregnant wife, Queen Aroha, back to her home of Tangala. Any day, the kingdom expected to hear the heir had been born. Left in charge, the young wizard Daltec sat on a simple chair, reading over reports from across the land. He rose from a low seat as they entered, his youthful face worried.

"You bear ill tidings, Captain," said Daltec, touching his own forehead. "I saw your coming as a darkness in my mind."

Captain Harkman bowed to the throne then stood facing Daltec, his hand resting on the hilt of his sword. "My search parties have not found Berric," he reported. "I believe it is time to recall the soldiers to the City. Guarding the Royal Palace should be our priority."

Read

GRYMON THE BITING HORROR

to find out what happens next!

Fight the Beasts, Fear the Magic

Do you want to know more about BEAST QUEST?
Then join our Quest Club!

Visit
www.beastquest.co.uk/club
and sign up today!

Are you a collector of the Beast Quest Cards?
Visit the website for further information.

MEET TEAM HERO
FROM ADAM BLADE
THEIR GIFTS MAKE THEM DIFFERENT
NICE HANDS!
FREAK!
BUT WHEN DANGER COMES...
CRACK!
RUMBLE!
SCREEECH!
...A HERO IS BORN
OTHERS WITH GIFTS WILL SEEK THEM OUT...
...AND SHOW THEM THEIR DESTINY.
EVER HEARD OF HERO ACADEMY?
OUT NOW!
ADAM BLADE
TEAM HERO
BATTLE FOR THE SHADOW SWORD
ADAM BLADE
TEAM HERO
ATTACK OF THE BAT ARMY
ADAM BLADE
TEAM HERO
REPTILE REAWAKENED
ADAM BLADE
TEAM HERO
THE SKELETON WARRIOR
TEAMHEROBOOKS.CO.UK
DARE TO BE DIFFERENT
JUN 2018

Jubilee

Houghton Mifflin Literary Fellowship Awards

E. P. O'Donnell, *Green Margins*
Dorothy Baker, *Young Man with a Horn*
Robert Penn Warren, *Night Rider*
Joseph Wechsberg, *Looking for a Bluebird*
Ann Petry, *The Street*
Elizabeth Bishop, *North & South*
Anthony West, *The Vintage*
Arthur Mizener, *The Far Side of Paradise*
Madison A. Cooper, Jr., *Sironia, Texas*
Charles Bracelen Flood, *Love Is a Bridge*
Milton Lott, *The Last Hunt*
Eugene Burdick, *The Ninth Wave*
Philip Roth, *Goodbye, Columbus*
William Brammer, *The Gay Place*
Clancy Sigal, *Going Away*
Edward Hoagland, *The Cat Man*
Ellen Douglas, *A Family's Affairs*
John Stewart Carter, *Full Fathom Five*
Margaret Walker, *Jubilee*
Berry Morgan, *Pursuit*
Robert Stone, *A Hall of Mirrors*
Willie Morris, *North Toward Home*
Georgia McKinley, *Follow the Running Grass*
Elizabeth Cullinan, *House of Gold*
Edward Hannibal, *Chocolate Days, Popsicle Weeks*
Helen Yglesias, *How She Died*
Henry Bromell, *The Slightest Distance*
Julia Markus, *Uncle*
Jean Strouse, *Alice James*
Patricia Hampl, *A Romantic Education*
W. P. Kinsella, *Shoeless Joe*
David Payne, *Confessions of a Taoist on Wall Street*
Ethan Canin, *Emperor of the Air*
David Campbell, *The Crystal Desert*
Ashley Warlick, *The Distance from the Heart of Things*

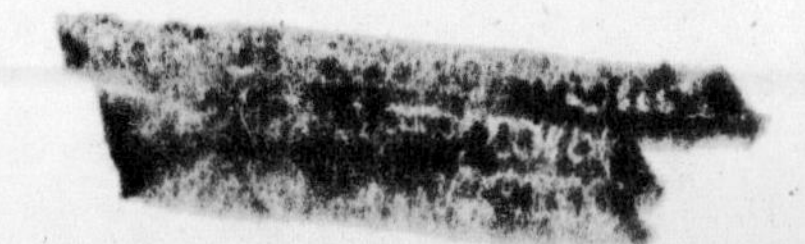